The Little Old Man Who Could Not Read

Irma Simonton Black · Pictures by Seymour Fleishman

Published by
READER'S DIGEST SERVICES, INC.
Pleasantville, New York

*For my daughter, Constance Black Engle,
and her family. I.S.B.*

2nd printing ....March 1976

Printed in U.S.A.

Once there was a little old man
who could not read.
He just never wanted to learn.
His wife went to the store
and bought the food
      but—

—the little man stayed home and
made beautiful toys out of wood.
Children all over the world
loved his toys, and many wrote
to tell him so.
But *still*
the little old man
never wanted
to learn
to read.

One day his wife decided to go
on a visit.
"You will need to go to the store,"
she said.
"Get a can of soup,
     and a big can of spaghetti sauce
     and some spaghetti.
Get some sugar
     and some milk
     and some oatmeal.
Eat well!"
And she kissed the old man and left.

The old man
went to the store.
There were rows
and rows of cans
with pictures on them.

And there were rows and rows
of cans and boxes without pictures.

What were they?
The little man did not know,
and he didn't like to ask.

He bought a middle-sized can.
It looked like the cans of soup
his wife brought home.

He bought a long box
that looked like
a spaghetti box
and a big can
that looked like
a spaghetti sauce can.

He bought a blue box that
looked like a sugar box.
He bought a round box that
looked like an oatmeal box.

And, last of all, he bought
a square carton.
It looked like the milk cartons
his wife brought home.

"Ah!" said the little old man
when he got home.
"That walk made me hungry.
I shall have some hot soup for lunch."

He opened the middle-sized can. It was onion soup.
The little old man
hated onions
of any kind—
and onion soup
worst of all.
"Fiddle," he said.
"*Onion* soup.
I shall save it
for my good wife."

At dinnertime, the little old man
rubbed his hands with pleasure
and took down the long box that
looked like a spaghetti box
and the great big can that
looked like a spaghetti sauce can.

Beaming, he opened the long box.
But the box did not have spaghetti in it.
It had wax paper.

"Fiddlesticks and fish fur!"
said the little old man.
"Who wants to eat
wax paper —
even with sauce on it?
Not I, for one.
But I can eat the sauce
all by itself."

He reached for the big can.
For the first time, he noticed
that it had a plastic top on it,
so he took that off.
"That's funny," he said to himself.
"I never saw a plastic top
 on a sauce can.
I do hope this isn't a coffee can!"

He opened the big can.
It *was* a coffee can.
The coffee smelled delicious,
but it wasn't much good
for a hungry little old man.

"Shall I have my oatmeal
and milk and sugar instead?"
he asked himself.
Then he answered himself.
"No, I'll have a cup of coffee
and go to bed. In the morning I'll have
a nice big breakfast."

By the next morning, he was very,
    very hungry.
"Oatmeal!" said the old man
as he jumped out of bed.
"I shall put lots and lots
of milk and sugar on it. Ah!"

The little old man got the round box
     and the blue box
          and the square carton.
He put them all on the table.
Then he opened the round box.

There was no oatmeal in it.
It was full of something
grainy and white.
The old man tasted it carefully.

Salt!
"Fiddles and flutes," said the old man.
"Who wants milk and sugar on *salt?*"

He opened the blue box and got a spoon
to have a sweet taste of sugar.
But there was no sugar in the box.
It was full of little white flakes.
"Soap!" said the old man sadly.
"Who wants soap even with milk?
Oh, oh, how hungry I am!"

He opened the square carton
to get a drink of milk.
But the milk in the carton
smelled funny.
It was buttermilk,
sour, *sour* buttermilk.
The old man
hated buttermilk, but
he was so hungry
that he drank
every drop of it.

The old man hated onion soup.
But at noon he was so hungry that
he ate the onion soup.

At night the wife came back.

The old man was very glad to see her.

"Wife," he said, "I had a bad time."

He told her how he got all mixed up
with the cans
and cartons
and boxes.

"The long box was not spaghetti.
It was wax paper!

The blue box was soap flakes!
The round box was salt!
Wife, please teach me to read!"

"Very well, I shall," said his good wife.
First the old man
learned to read the word
  spaghetti.
Next he learned to read the word
  milk.

Then he learned to read the words
for everything in the big store.
And then he learned to read the words
for everything in the world.

But he still made his beautiful toys
out of wood,
    and now he could read
the letters the children sent to him.
And he never—no, never—went hungry again.